KINDERGATORS

Miracle Melts Down

· ·

ROSEMARY WELLS

KATHERINE TEGEN BOOKS

An Imprint of HarperCollins Publishers

Well, Miracle came to school with a supersize pack of Fudgettes in her pocket. She didn't tell anyone about them.

You know how Miss Harmony says, "Bring it to school, bring it to share"? Do you think Miracle wanted to share even one Fudgette?

No way, José! She went back and forth and back and forth and back and forth to pop a Fudgette into her mouth.

Miss Harmony rang her "good morning" bell and Friendly Circle sat down.

But Miracle kept asking to go to the girls' room. (She was really heading to the coat closet. That's where she hid the bag of Fudgettes!)

And you know how Miss Harmony always says, "Only healthy snacks in school"? Miracle knows Fudgettes are not even a little bit healthy.

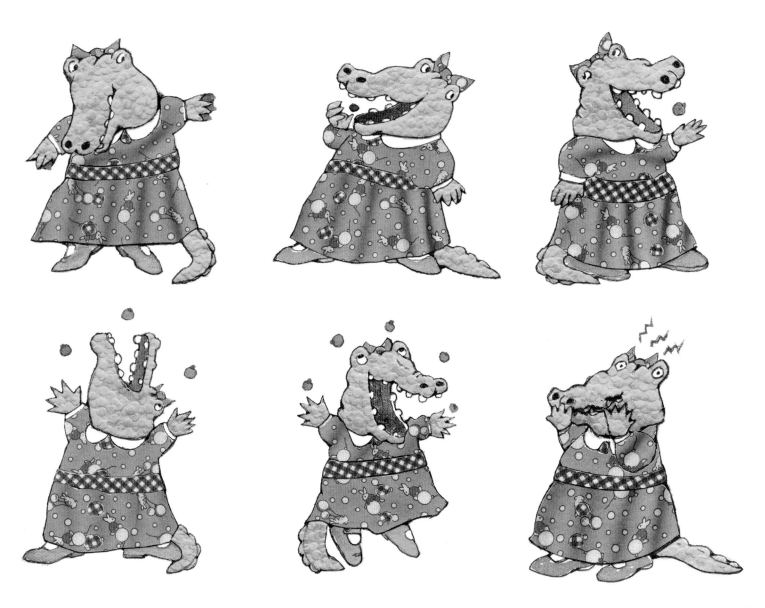

Everyone thinks Fudgettes give you the "sugar crazies," but Miracle ate them anyway.

Miss Harmony wanted to know why Miracle needed to go to the girls' room 270 times in a row.

"Are you feeling well, Miracle?" asked Miss Harmony.

"Oh, I'm fine, fine, fine!" answered Miracle.

Just then, Miracle's luck ran out.

Her raincoat was hanging right over the radiator!

And all of her Fudgettes had melted into one big chocolate blob.

Knock! Knock! Knock! went Miss Harmony on the girls' room door.
Miracle melted down under one of the sinks.

Miracle would not stop crying.

"Let's sing the 'Feel Better' song to Miracle," said Miss Harmony.

Miracle, Miracle, you're so sweet,
From your head down to your feet!
You're so bumpy, you're so green,
The nicest gator we've ever seen!

Miracle went through half a box of tissues because of
the Fudgette meltdown. Everyone tried to help.
"She needs a jeweled necklace!" said Babette.
"How about a Queen for the Day crown?" asked Nigel.
Miracle felt beautiful until lunchtime.

Today was tuna salad day.

Miracle hated the celery bits in tuna salad, so she tried to take them out of her sandwich but the sandwich fell apart.

Miracle fell apart too, right there at the lunch table.
Her grape juice tipped over.
"Never mind, we'll clean up!" said Babette.

"You can have my apple!" offered Raúl.

Miracle was all smiles until after lunch.

Then Miss Harmony said, "Counting Card time! Who's our leader?"

"My turn!" said Miracle. "My turn! My turn!"

But it wasn't Miracle's turn. It was Jazzmin's turn to be Counting Card leader.
"What's the number on my card?" asked Jazzmin.
Everybody answered but Miracle.

Miss Harmony said, "Miracle, your name comes in the middle of the Take Turns banner, just the way the alphabet goes."

But Miracle wanted to be first. She went into full meltdown again!

Then Miss Harmony called Friendly Circle into emergency session.
"We need to put on our thinking caps, everyone!" said Miss Harmony.
Jazzmin suggested applying the cooling mask to Miracle's eyes.

Nigel thought Miracle needed the Calm Down with Mozart music.
"Let me explain the Take Turns banner, Miracle," said Babette.
But it was Miguel who found a solution.
"Line dancing will make Miracle happy again," said Miguel.

Miss Harmony played "Ragtime Gator's Ball."

One step left, two steps right,
Clap and turn on a Saturday night.
Wiggle for a nickel, wiggle for a dime . . .
Forward, turn around, one more time.

Suddenly Miguel stepped on Miracle's foot.
"Ow!!!!!!!" shouted Miracle.
"Ow!
          Ow!
                OW!"

Miracle's eyes got very, very big.

Miracle's mouth got very, very twitchy.

"I know!" said Tina. She ran for the Counting Cards.

"Take 'em," said Jazzmin. "Hurry!"

"Your turn to count to ten,
Miracle," said Tina.
"One . . ." Miracle whispered.

Miracle counted all of the cards.

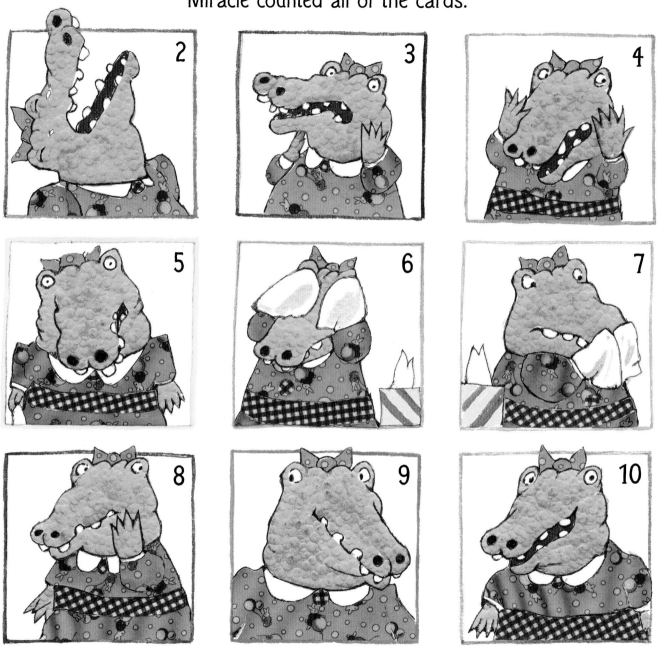

By the time Miracle had counted to ten, she was calm again.
There were no sniffles, no tears, no howls!

"It's a Miracle!" said Miss Harmony.
Everyone cheered.

At see-you-later-alligator time, Miss Harmony gave Miracle
the Star of Bravery to wear home.

"With this star I'll never melt down again!" said Miracle.

Everybody line-danced home.

"And that's what happened
at school today!"

Creating Harmony

One of the big challenges teachers face is creating classroom harmony.

Harmony means that all students can learn, be heard, and feel safe among their classmates. This is no easy goal, but the Kindergators books help show how one child's behavior affects everyone in a group.

Practicing empathy helps to create harmony. Encouragement, examples, and classroom discussions can help.

Here are a few conversation starters:

- What is something that makes you frustrated or upset?
- What can be done to dry the tears and make the smiles come out again?
- How did Miracle's classmates feel when she screamed about each little thing that went wrong?
- How did the Kindergators get together and fix Miracle's bad day?

Families can help by understanding what causes frequent meltdowns in a child, so the next time everyone can be prepared to cope. Redirecting a melter-down's attention works. Encouraging a child to speak up about his or her true feelings, even if he or she is embarrassed or frightened by emotions, also works. Knowing what they really feel helps youngsters get control when they start to cry.

Here are a few of Miss Harmony's helpful hints to diffuse a crisis:

1. Count to ten.

2. Go away by yourself until the crying stops.

3. Eat or drink something.

4. Take ten deep breaths, letting them out slowly.

Thank you,
Johanna Hurley!

Thanks to Windham Fabrics, Maywood Studio Fabrics, RJR Fabrics, Moda Fabrics, Darlene Zimmerman, Judy Rothermel, Kaye England, and Barbara Brackman.

Katherine Tegen Books is an imprint of HarperCollins Publishers.

Library of Congress Cataloging-in-Publication Data is available.
ISBN 978-0-06-192115-5

Typography by Rachel Zegar   12 13 14 15 16   SCP   10 9 8 7 6 5 4 3 2 1 ❖ First Edition

Babette · Benjamin · Harry · Jazzmin · Lola